Renier-Fréduman Mundil

Uhlenspiegel with the Schilda Citizens

Uhle 2 (Volume 2)

AF191041

Renier-Fréduman Mundil

Uhlenspiegel with the Schilda Citizens

Uhle 2

Translated from German

by Hilary Teske

Bibliographic information from the German National Library:
The German National Library lists this publication in the
German National Bibliography; detailed bibliographic data is
available online at http://dnb.dnb.de.

All rights reserved
© 2025 Renier-Fréduman Mundil, Viola Hartmann
Cover design: Dan Winkler
Editing: Malin Friese
Publisher: BoD · Books on Demand GmbH, Überseering 33, 22297
Hamburg, bod@bod.de Print: Libri Plureos GmbH, Friedensallee
273, 22763 Hamburg

ISBN: 978-3-8192-9869-1

For
Samuel Friedrich

Introduction

On sense and nonsense or on the sense of senselessness or on the sense of nonsense.

One foolishness is not good, two foolishnesses are not necessarily better, unless they try to out(trump) each other negatively or, to put it another way, they try to compensate for each other, a kind of upside-down complete compensation deal in such a way that both decompensate in the sense of not becoming even worse but disappearing together in unison.

Whether that makes sense remains to be seen. But sense is one of those things. Even in nonsense there is at least (linguistically) sense, to a certain extent the sense of not making sense, not andsense but nonsense.

Why has language never invented the word andsense? Hard to explain! Because in a common, pardon, hardly general way there are sometimes two senses in one thing. We are quite content to find one sense in a thing; at most, by using all our senses, it may be possible to elicit several senses from a thing, the sense of touch to be felt, the sense of hearing to be heard, a sense of feeling that cannot be grasped, and so on.

But all this seems senseless (or senseLess, perhaps Sense(less)).

SenseLess, the sense is perhaps a lot as in a draw, sometimes to be found in a thing, often not, just like a lot. (Translator's note: this is a play on the German word 'los' which means 'less' and 'lot in a draw' but it can't be translated directly into English).

Sense-less. That makes more sense. Someone has unhooked the sense of a thing, like you unhook a moored boat, and both sense and boat are soon gone. A boating sense, if that makes any sense. Still there but gone, just no longer there, pardon no longer here but (somewhere) still there.

So if something is sense less, pardon, senseless, that is, without sense, how can it make double sense? A nothing can hardly be doubled, something that is senseless can hardly be doubly senseless, more senseless. Senseless can only mean that the sense is no longer so solid, will soon disappear, be completely gone and haste is required to grasp it before it is even more loose, completely loose, that is, completely gone.

Senseless, that is, something without sense and in a double sense. Does that make (at least one(1)) sense? To make one out of nothing would be a magic trick, to make one out of a double sense would be an inestimable loss. A sense of loss, pardon a loss of sense.

This digression made little sense, perhaps even no sense at all.

Senseless, double sense? That makes no sense at all. Why would it make sense to look twice at something that doesn't even exist?

An empty plate doesn't get any fuller if we look at it twice. And it is absolutely senseless or absurd or even nonsensical to look twice at something that is not there. At some point, we (or our senses) will think that we have been deceived, that we (via the sometimes senseless path of our senses) have tricked ourselves, so to speak.

In a figurative sense, there is something of these thoughts in the following stories.

Two main protagonists – the lone fighter Uhlenspiegel, but with the army of his mischievous thoughts – meets the armies of the numerous Schilda citizens (rather less or let's say more neutrally armed with other thoughts).

Is such an encounter sensible? Is it perhaps senseless? Or does it perhaps make at least double sense, an and-sense, if not multiple sense?

All this remains open, just as we should go through life with open senses in order to recognize what makes sense or even to discover a hidden sense in an adventurous way - to find out where there is a (the) sense or whether it is simply missing, a kind of non-sense and in this sense as non-sense even less than nonsense, which exists somewhere, otherwise it would not be nonsense.

To summarize or to sum up the sense: everyone has to find out for themselves whether it makes sense to read these stories or to bring Uhlenspiegel together with a village of Schilda citizens. That in turn would then make sense. In this way, every reader would make sense of these stories (pardon interpret sense into them) where there was no sense before and it would have made sense (for everyone) to write or read these stories.

However, they should approach the sense and nonsense of these stories unencumbered (meaning already encumbered with sense but equipped with unencumbered senses).

With this in mind: lots of sense enjoyment.

*PS.1: Topical note

Perhaps this explains the phenomenon of dictatorships that is emerging again today. A single person (but with almost absolutely immovable sense) is confronted with a huge mass of people whose senses are rather dulled. A constellation that not only makes no sense, but makes (pardon contains) an incredibly dangerous sense. More than nonsense, much more, the strongest nonsense there can ever be.

PS.2: Reading recommendation

It may make sense to read only one story a month, or it may not make sense to read more than one story a month. That's why this book contains twelve stories. If you feel like reading more, you can of course read all twelve stories in one day instead of just one story a month.

You will want to get to the stories at last. Here you go. Have fun.

1.
Dangerous dream of gold

$\mathcal{A}$s fate would have it, Uhlenspiegel was burdened with a serious illness. When he finally recovered after many weeks, he realized that not only the illness was gone, but also all the money he had worked so hard to obtain by trickery. Now the illness had had something to do with his stomach, and as Uhlenspiegel understood so much about medicine, a stomach has no hands and feet, it could not possibly have been the illness itself that had carried the money away. The only remaining cause of the disappearance was the quack doctor who had treated Uhlenspiegel and had been paid a princely sum for it.

If I have gone through stomach disease myself, I now know how to cure it, Uhlenspiegel thought. No other profession – he was thinking of the quacks – seemed more suitable for him to regain possession of a small fortune and, on top of that, it didn't seem to matter to him how an illness was treated, it lasted just as long with medicine as without, only illnesses put people in strange states in which they wanted to be treated with martial methods and stuffed with bitter medicine like a goose.

The first thing Uhlenspiegel did was to write himself a few decent references regarding his reputation. He invented all sorts of strange names, of emperors who lived in China, Arabia and elsewhere and attested to him in strange characters that he had repeatedly snatched them from the clutches of a deadly disease. They also deeply regretted that he intended to return to his homeland and was therefore unable to remain their imperial physician any longer.

Nevertheless, they offered him the opportunity to return at any time and take up his old position, even if he was old, blind and deaf, for even in such a state there could be no better physician in the whole world than him.

Thus, equipped and clad in suitable clothing, Uhlenspiegel set off for Schilda. Fate meant well with him, or perhaps fate had a guilty conscience because of the serious illness it had saddled him with.

On the market square, Uhlenspiegel saw a man sitting and begging who seemed strange to him. Both his legs and his arms were wrapped in white bandages, and he just had his fingers free to hold a hat for collecting coins. Every now and then a citizen of Schilda would stop and throw a little money into the hat.

Uhlenspiegel positioned himself in front of the poor devil and shouted so that he could be heard all over the marketplace, asking if he wanted him, a well-traveled and experienced doctor, to help him.

The beggar nodded: Of course, he would like nothing better than to be able to stand on his own two feet again and work with his own hands instead of sitting day in, day out as a miserable creature in the marketplace, dependent on the alms of others.

Uhlenspiegel, however, thought he saw through him, that it was nothing more than that he had made himself comfortable, earning his money in a pleasant spot in the sun and in a comfortable seat, on top of having his food brought to him and being carried back and forth in the morning and evening like an emperor in a sedan chair. In the meantime, a good crowd of onlookers had gathered, just as Uhlenspiegel had intended.

He raised his hands imploringly over the sick man, mumbled a few unintelligible words, reached into his pocket and told the man to take the medicine. In a moment, however, he would recover and be able to walk on his own feet again, which is what every human being is given to do.

The beggar swallowed the medicine and everyone stared at him with wide, staring eyes. Everyone had their ailments, if the poor devil actually jumped up it should be easy for the strange doctor to cure them of their far more significant ailments, even if they seemed far less serious on the outside.

Nothing happened. On the contrary. The patient seemed to be worse off than before.

Now Uhlenspiegel was beginning to get upset, as he thought he had an actor in front of him who was ruining his good business with money. He approached the beggar, leaned forward, said something about fair payment, grabbed the money-filled hat and ran off. You should have seen the beggar. He jumped up like the devil and rushed after him, his arms and legs still wrapped in white bandages, to get his money back.

When Uhlenspiegel saw this, he stopped. The beggar also stopped, only now realizing what had happened. Uhlenspiegel, however, took advantage of the moment and explained unctuously that it was easy for him to get a paralytic on his feet, as everyone had seen with their own eyes, and that he would be ready tomorrow to free everyone from their complaints.

But he put the money from the beggar's hat in his pocket, the payment was appropriate, not only had he cured the patient, he had also never seen anyone walk so fast, which had certainly not been possible to this extent before the illness. In a way, he had healed the patient.

But fate was doubly kind to Uhlenspiegel. At the time when he had performed his first miracle, the quack who had cured him and emptied his wallet was suffering from a terrible illness. The news of Uhlenspiegel's work reached him in no time at all and he sent for him to also benefit from his healing abilities.

Uhlenspiegel immediately made his way to the magnificent house where the quack was lying on his sickbed. What a pitiful state he was in. Uhlenspiegel would have been moved to pity had he not had to constantly think of his lost fortune.

He inquired about the nature of the illness, where and what kind of pain was present and where it was particularly noticeable. The quack pointed to his whole corpulent body, then he pointed to his back, where it was most painful at the moment, but this could be due to lying down for so long, as he had already been confined to bed for three days.

Uhlenspiegel reassured the patient, as he knew of an excellent, if somewhat laborious, treatment. He had a cage made with a round opening, just large enough, but still of considerable dimensions to fit the quack's buttocks. He then had a beehive brought in, placed the dear creatures in the cage, ordered the quack's backside to be coated with sugar and that he should then sit on the painstakingly made cage, with the aching part on the opening, and the bees would do the rest.

It helped, at least for Uhlenspiegel, every sting and every scream was satisfaction for his lost fortune. But the quack was no better. Even when his already impressive buttocks had swollen fourfold, the pain had by no means subsided.

Uhlenspiegel was ordered to remove him from the cage and take him back to bed. Two citizens of Schilda volunteered to help and brought the poor devil back. When Uhlenspiegel happened to look at the exposed, sugared buttocks of the sick man, he saw a bee still feasting on the sugar. Now he was overcome with pity, he reached out and kicked the insect so hard that it cracked. However, it was not the broken chitinous shell that had caused such a noise, rather Uhlenspiegel had accidentally hit the right spot, and the dislocated vertebra had sprung back into place.

The quack's face brightened. All the pain, and not just the back pain, was forgotten. Overjoyed, he threw his arms around Uhlenspiegel's neck. A second medical miracle had taken place in Schilda; it must truly be a great, important physician who, after long (unnecessary) journeys and service at the most exquisite courts in the world, deigned to heal the infirm in their tranquil Schilda. But there was still a lot more for Uhlenspiegel to do, even with the quack doctor, who was still in possession of Uhlenspiegel's fortune.

One night in Schilda, which was already dreaming all the time, the mayor was overcome by a strange dream. He saw himself sitting on a magnificent throne, adorned with both gold and precious stones, while emissaries from distant lands appeared to pay their respects.

Drenched in sweat, he woke up and suddenly summoned all the councilors. It was urgent to interpret the dream. It was possible that the first envoys were already on their way, which meant that the first of them could set foot in worldly Schilda at any moment.

Great importance was attached to the dream during the nightly council meeting. It was decided to triple the size of the town hall and to erect an even more magnificent throne in the middle of a magnificent hall. The mayor was to sit on this throne as emperor, as anyone who knew how to be an emperor in their dreams would find it easy to play the role in real life. All the jewelry in Schilda was collected for the precious throne and soon the women only looked like withered trees in autumn. As there were not enough stones to enlarge the town hall and there was also a need for haste, it was decided to demolish all the houses except for four corner pillars so that the roofs would not fall to the ground, because you had to have a roof over your head, otherwise there would be no need for a head.

The work was soon completed in an excellent manner. The mayor was placed on the throne and properly fattened up so that his already stately appearance was enhanced and worthy of an emperor. Full of impatience and excitement, the citizens of Schilda waited for the envoys who would come from all corners of the earth and bring splendid gifts to make up for the loss of the ornaments many times over.

The days passed, the tension grew, the impatience grew, the figure of the mayor grew. The latter at such a pace that a new, much wider throne would soon have to be made if the whole drama didn't come to a good end soon.

It was a good thing that Uhlenspiegel came along. He quickly saw through the buffoonery, and he also benefited from the fact that the citizens of Schilda regarded him as the first emissary, who came from the farthest end of the world no less, because of his strange clothing.

Uhlenspiegel let them have their way. After being courted for several days and being fed and clothed with all kinds of valuables, he grew tired of the comfort and decided that he should also have some fun.

When the Schilda Emperor began to talk again about the many envoys that were waiting in the wings, Uhlenspiegel looked at him reproachfully. Why hadn't he spoken about this problem earlier?

And if he didn't know that he, as a well-traveled, worldly bon vivant, had a solution to every problem, the right lid for the pot, so to speak. It had seemed strange to him on the journey. The area around Schilda was teeming with splendidly dressed, distinguished people wandering around aimlessly as if they were looking for something in particular. And now it would have occurred to him that the strangers were looking for nothing other than Schilda, where they could bring their splendid gifts, loaded on mules, horses, camels and even elephants. The mayor's eyes widened into a barn door. His nocturnal dream had not deceived him, nor had the drudgery of fattening up been in vain. Soon the strangers would be standing in an endless line in front of his throne, eager to be the first to do him honor.

But how could the strangers find their way to Schilda, the Schilda Emperor worriedly turned to Uhlenspiegel.

He also knew the answer.

Venerable Emperor of Schilda, he said. You and your court, including the last mouse in your realm, are certainly in a difficult situation. But fate has been kind to you in bringing me here at a time when your need is greatest. I must have seen many kingdoms on this earth, one more splendid than the next. None of them were lavish and flaunted their wealth so that every eye could enjoy it. This means nothing other than that you must collect all the gold coins. Melt down half of them and use them to gild the dome of the town hall. This way, the whole world, and especially the wandering emissaries, can see what an extraordinary place this forest is. However, it may happen that some emissaries wander hopelessly behind the hilltops and cannot even see the magnificent golden dome from there.

But you can't remove the mountains just so that your golden dome can be seen better. So give me the other half of the gold coins and I'll scatter them on all the paths that lead to your little town. Surely everyone can see straight away that there must be something special at the end of the paths paved with gold.

The Schilda Emperor was about to get up, but Uhlenspiegel told him to stay seated, as he had not yet finished his advice.

As I already stated on another occasion, the envoys are carrying precious gifts with them, which they have loaded on to all kinds of strange animals. Among them were camels, with three humps on their backs and an extra hump because of the many gifts. Just the kind of special camels that suit your court. However, as they have three humps themselves, these animals can only be moved along paths that lead over hills. You won't be able to tell the difference in the forest, but you will in your flat little town. So you have to make hills everywhere on the roads, otherwise you won't be able to get the camels to walk any further and you won't get to the precious gifts they carry between their humps.

When Uhlenspiegel saw the horrified faces, he decided to add a little extra.

Other deputies are carrying huge elephants, which are four walking columns with a water hose in front of them, and this enormous walking structure would otherwise not be able to transport the many gifts. Now these pachyderms, especially when they come out of the cool forest into the heat of a big busy city like Schilda, are used to taking a cool mud bath every 50 meters. Where you have not raised any hills, you must diligently dig deep holes in your streets and fill them with water. It works well together, because if you dig the holes, you will have enough sand for the camel mounds.

I will stay with you at the beginning to make sure that the hills are high enough and the holes are deep enough. None of you know such strange animals and I can assure you that their demands are just as high as those of the imperial court that sent them. But once I have seen enough that you are doing the job wisely and correctly, I must set off to scatter the gold coins. But soon, and Uhlenspiegel looked at the Schilda Emperor for a second, you will have more than one elephant in your city and a great many more camels (than you have now, he thought to himself, but better not say it).

It happened just as Uhlenspiegel had guessed. After he had had his fill of digging holes and raising hills, he had an ox cart hitched up and made off with half the gold coins. The golden dome of Schilda could still be seen for a long time, like a picture from a thousand and one nights, from a peaceful paradise, albeit with ups and downs along the way, but without a single gold coin; what an oasis of happiness, wasn't money the root of all evil in the world?

And in this way, Uhlenspiegel had also cured the quack of this evil in passing, for this kind of profession often possesses most of this evil and this kind of cure meant nothing other than that Uhlenspiegel had recovered his lost small fortune from the quack, even if by a somewhat strange route. Of course, he only scattered this fortune that had returned to him, as well as the other gold coins entrusted to him, in golden thoughts along the paths that led to tranquil Schilda.

2.
Nothing (-) makes you happy

When the first citizens of Schilda had once again ventured out of their tranquil town into the unknown world and then returned, gloom descended on Schilda. They had realized that they had lost their uniqueness, because all the strange things that could only be found in Schilda had found their way into the world.

Robbed of their uniqueness, the citizens of Schilda fell into a deeply depressed mood. In this state, they also suffered the fate of Uhlenspiegel coming to their town. It did not take long for him to recognize their grief, and he was immediately ready to remedy this terrible plight.

He had traveled the world a lot, Uhlenspiegel explained, and could confirm that he had discovered similar works of art all over the world, such as houses without windows, leaning buildings that looked as if they would topple over the next moment and a colorfulness that would make even a clown pale with envy in its splendor of color. Unfortunately, no one had dared to ask them, the citizens of Schilda, whether they were allowed to imitate such artful things, these very houses or the transportation of light in sacks, after all, the citizens of Schilda were the originators of all these achievements, which were certainly difficult to imagine.

Don't worry, he still didn't think that the world out there was happy. This could mean nothing other than that everything out there did not contribute to happiness.

The solution was therefore so simple: all you had to do was give up everything you knew, and you would regain your uniqueness and happiness to boot. Now the whole thing is not that simple, after all, you simply or admittedly often cannot do without everything.

Out there, people were walking around on legs, and you shouldn't think that everyone in Schilda should give up their legs, go to the nearest butcher, have them cut off and experience happiness that way. They would certainly be the only city in the whole world where everyone walked around without legs and would have created something new and unique. But only uniqueness and not happiness.

It was the same with thinking, eyes, breathing, with everything, so he, Uhlenspiegel, as an expert on happiness, was needed to sort out where and what everyone in Schilda should do without in order to find happiness again.

The first thing was to do without such trivial things as tables, chairs and beds. He had traveled all over the world, even to places where no one had ever set foot. He had never found such things as tables, chairs and beds anywhere in nature, and yet the plants and animals seemed particularly happy in these places. And elsewhere in the world, where there was an abundance of tables, beds and chairs, so that every corner was filled with them, he could find no happiness among people.

So put all the chairs, tables and beds on top of each other in a huge pyramid. This will get rid of these annoying things, give you a new work of art and give happiness enough space to return to your homes. When you have had your fill of this pyramid of abundance, set it on fire so that these things also disappear from your minds as images. For this is also an art; to create art and then let the art itself and the images of this art disappear from your minds again.

Not everyone liked the idea, but it made sense to the sensible citizens of Schilda. They regained some of their uniqueness, but despite the lack of chairs, tables and beds, they were not happy. Uhlenspiegel took a look at their misfortune and realized that they had not carried out his advice thoroughly enough.

The many tables and chairs were still standing around in the town hall and Uhlenspiegel told them that they needed to remedy this problem quickly if they were to finally achieve the desired success. It happened and the effect was not lost. As soon as all the tables and chairs had been removed, the faces of the citizens brightened. They no longer received official mail, because how could such things be done without a table and chair? They were no longer summoned to the big, horrible building with the dark eyes to fill out superfluous applications and forms, because there was nowhere to sit down, no table to write on.

When Uhlenspiegel saw the first success and how happiness began to return to the faces of the citizens of Schilda, he thought the opportunity was favorable to go one better, to perfect the happiness of the citizens of Schilda.

Citizens of Schilda, he said, I now see you equipped with sufficient understanding to take the final step towards attaining complete happiness. Have you never thought about the annoyances you have to thank your hands for? They make you do inexplicable things from morning till night, they do things that annoy your neighbor or even cause you grief when they take something from others.

This should be remedied, not in a drastic form, as he had already seen on his journey through the world. On his many journeys, he had occasionally come across people with their hands clasped behind their backs and walking back and forth, or with their hands buried in their pockets, standing around and observing their surroundings, beaming with happiness. Now it must be clear to the last person why these people are incomparably happy. In such a state, you can't do anything with your hands that brings unhappiness to your face – work, theft, anger and the like.

Tie your hands behind your back and walk around your tranquil little town all day long. Or put a lump of gold in your trouser pocket and hold it in your fist so that your hand can't get out of your pocket to do things that will only bring misfortune to your face. But before that, I must explain to you in passing that the fear of losing something you own usually causes great worry, so it is better to give such things away, because afterwards you will certainly not be able to lose them and will have no reason to carry worry around in your face. So, throw your money on the street so that it no longer brings worry to your face. Doesn't it mean happiness when your money is on the street? And while you go for a walk with your hands tied, I will subject myself to the work and misfortune of sweeping up the money so that you can walk along clean paths, also so that you don't trip over the money or even slip like on an ice rink, because quite a few people know how slippery money is.

So, you see that I myself am willing to take on a heavy burden so that from now on you may gain your old reputation in a happy uniqueness and the foreign, distant world will speak of you with respect, even a little envy, when it hears of your happy state and learns of the other circumstances.

3.
Money stinks (doesn't stink)

*U*hlenspiegel had been lazing around for six months and was slowly growing tired of being lazy. The memory of the tranquil little town of Schilda, where the world was still in simple order, came just at the right time. There was no suspicion, no resentment, no deceit, just the guileless, innocent, simple belief that things were as they should be and that everything was in a simple, manageable order. The memory of the citizens of Schilda came just in time for Uhlenspiegel, as his own purse was empty and the larder was a huge black hole and, to make matters worse, winter was already knocking on the leaky door.

Dressed like a man of the world, Uhlenspiegel set off. In his hand he carried a golden suitcase filled with all kinds of cleaning utensils.

After a few days, he saw the spire of the Schilda church. He felt happy and warm in his heart, as if the sunken El Dorado had risen overnight from a subterranean labyrinth of the earth. The wooden pedestal on which he used to stand was still there on the market square – not without placing the golden suitcase in the red evening glow of the setting sun. The bait did not fail to have its effect; like a meat magnet, it attracted the dull citizens of Schilda, who flocked out of their houses on to the market square in droves.

Forgive me if my golden suitcase dazzles you, Uhlenspiegel began his wondrous speech. But I accidentally placed it against the wall of my house, and since it is made of pure gold, the poor suitcase had no choice but to pick up some of the shiny metal.

The citizens of Schilda were quite astonished at this message. A house made of gold didn't seem like a bad place to live in. And once the real hardship of life had caught up with you, all you had to do was break out a piece of gold in an unimportant place and give hardship a good kick up the backside.

Uhlenspiegel noticed how the first ones were nibbling at the bait. A quick tug at the right moment and enough inhabitants of Schilda would be wriggling irretrievably on his line.

Money doesn't stink, said Uhlenspiegel. I think every one of you knows that saying. But nobody will know that it comes from me, that it can only come from me. Because I am the only one who, on his many travels around the world, has held every coin in his hand once to judge that not a single one of the infinite number of coins stinks.

Just don't take it for granted that money doesn't stink. It's not the hard work one does that is the hard part about money. That is child's play compared to the hard work of washing the money so that it no longer stinks. For this is how all the coins in the wide world were handled before they came into my hands for a high-level examination of their purity, for word of my expert knowledge had long since spread to the four corners of the earth. That is why I have come. Where do you put your money? In your trouser pockets and thus very close to various openings that do not always smell good. But I offer to wash your money so that it will smell better than the most expensive perfume in Paris. It was for this very purpose that I brought my little golden suitcase, which I have already used to help many other people in this wide world.

Soon afterwards, the citizens of Schilda brought buckets of their money, which they had previously hidden in musty savings stockings and even mustier mattresses. Uhlenspiegel collected everything in a huge sack and told the citizens of Schilda to come back in two days. And there was a big surprise waiting for them. Two days ago, Uhlenspiegel's sack was full to bursting, but now the bottom half was bulging limply.

You've done me quite a job, Uhlenspiegel scolded. Your money was so dirty that it took me two sleepless nights to clean it. And when all the dirt was scrubbed away, all that was left was this.

However, Uhlenspiegel had done nothing more than tip the small half of the money into a baker's mixing trough, add a bottle of fine perfume and leave the whole thing to its own devices for two days.

I have traveled a lot, continued Uhlenspiegel, and on my travels I have come across a city in which everyone floats around all day long grinning like honey cakes out of pure joie de vivre. I eagerly struggled to uncover the secret.

The solution was so ridiculously simple that you almost stumbled over it.

In this city, the money was lying on the street, Uhlenspiegel continued. Nothing more and nothing less was the reason for their joie de vivre. And if you don't believe it, all you have to do is throw your money on the ground and take a few steps over it to experience this feeling of happiness in the flesh.

Even the citizens of Schilda understood this. But before this blissful state could be achieved, care had to be taken to ensure that the money reached the streets.

You certainly won't be dumping dirt on your streets, Uhlenspiegel interrupted their musings. I have also laundered your dirty money for this purpose. Now go home after I've returned the money to you and throw handfuls of it out of the window. Then the money will be lying on your streets tomorrow and you can walk through your city, even through your whole life, with your head held high and on the wings of happiness, like the well-born emperor of China. Remember, however, that I did not launder the money for you to throw it on dirty streets. You must first spend the day cleaning the streets so that they shine better than the table from which you eat your lunch. Only after this work will you return home and proceed as I have explained to you.

Uhlenspiegel had hardly spoken when he opened the sack and hurled the contents in a high arc across the marketplace. The result was a chaotic mess, the likes of which tranquil Schilda had never seen before. After the last grain of gold had been uncovered by the citizens amid the dirt and commotion, they returned to their homes, not a few of them with thick scratches and even thicker bruises and bloodshot eyes.

No sooner said than done. The streets and sidewalks were cleaned so that the sun could be seen in them as in an imperial mirror. In the evening, in the glow of the setting sun, which also shone on Uhlenspiegel's golden suitcase, the citizens of Schilda opened their windows and threw out the money. Then they lay down, expectant like little children on the last night before Christmas Day and dreamed themselves into their happiness.

Uhlenspiegel, however, collected the other half of the money during the night by sweeping every street even more thoroughly than the citizens of Schilda had done before. Never before had the streets of a small town been swept so sparkling clean and free of even the tiniest speck of dust. Satisfied, Uhlenspiegel made his way home. Winter could now come, including the frost, the storm and the ice. All that money seemed stronger to him than all those forces of nature that were about to descend on the tranquil, peaceful world.

4.
White/wise portable stoves

*T*he citizens of Schilda lived in tranquility, far away from the hectic hustle and bustle that surrounded them. The houses were small but smartly kept, the animals spruced up daily as if to win an animal Miss Universe contest, the streets polished like a king's silverware.

As the year changed, from the cozy mildness of summer to the uncomfortable stormy days of autumn and the frosty sounds of winter, the houses began to get comfortably warm in good time. Heated by coal and wood, the chimneys visible from afar puffed away. It was just as the people of Schilda wanted, everything was in order, the chimneys had even been extended with long pipes so that the smoke could rise as long as possible in a straight, orderly line into the sky. And it did, more and more each day, as the winter every day added an extra scoop of frost, which had to be resisted.

However, it soon became apparent that the houses were far better off than the people. The houses seemed to be quite comfortable, glowing with warmth and radiating an untouchable peace, which could only be due to the stoves. It was completely different with the people. Even though their breath smoked like a chimney in the cold mornings, they didn't feel nearly as comfortable. This was nothing less than a great injustice, as things should at least be on an equal footing between houses and people. This had to be remedied. But in what way? You couldn't just stuff wood and coal into the stoves, light them and wait for it to get cozy.

It just so happened that Uhlenspiegel was passing through the village again. He had actually only intended to use it to pass through, to shorten his journey to his actual destination. It only took a few steps in the village to notice the unhappy state of the inhabitants. And it took even fewer steps to find a solution, because Uhlenspiegel was used to coming up with solutions, albeit unusual ones, to difficulties.

Why, my dear citizens of Schilda, he began his contrived speech, why do you walk around like sourpusses? Of course, because you let your houses fare better than yourselves. Heat them with wood that has been laboriously brought in so that the doors, windows and walls are comfortable. And yourselves? As long as you are indoors, you can divert a little welfare to yourselves. But once you're outside, what then? You can't put the warmth in bags like the light or hide it under your clothes, trusting that the warmth will stick to you like saliva to your mouth. Why don't you do the same with yourselves as you do with your houses? Get yourself a stove, preferably one that you can carry around with you so that it heats you up wherever you are.

He pulled out something long, white on the outside like freshly fallen snow, dirty on the inside like a worn road. He put this strange thing in his mouth, lit it and soon began to smoke like a chimney himself. The citizens of Schilda were quite astonished, as they had never seen anyone set fire to themselves before.

You don't have to worry about burning yourselves, Uhlenspiegel reassured them. The warm smoke will warm you inside and out, but if the fire gets too close to you it will go out, at least most of the time, for fear of being eaten by your mouth.

The citizens of Schilda understood this. Uhlenspiegel was immediately prepared to give away such portable stoves for a small fee and promised to get more if needed.

After a while, all the citizens of Schilda were walking around with these smoking white sticks. It is said that some people tried to put them in other openings of their bodies, as it didn't seem to matter where the heat came in and if they used openings further down, their feet would also be warmed up better, as it was usually these parts of the body that felt the cold the most.

Uhlenspiegel had now made a good profit from the matter, but had not yet had his fun, which annoyed him despite his great earnings.

He therefore took the trouble to visit each individual and, under the seal of secrecy, tell them about the danger of the stoves he had introduced. He did not want to proclaim it to everyone, so as not to cause panic, and it was enough if only the person he approached knew the danger he was presenting to him, as he was particularly close to Uhlenspiegel's heart.

After Uhlenspiegel had made his rounds and every citizen of Schilda thought he was the only one in on the secret of the danger, Uhlenspiegel decided to leave the town. But only officially; in reality, he hid in disguise in every possible corner and was pleased to see buckets filled with water everywhere in Schilda. If a citizen of Schilda happened to pass by with this strange portable stove stuck in his mouth, Uhlenspiegel would blow a whistle, which meant to the next best person that the danger Uhlenspiegel had told him about was approaching. As a result, the man startled by the whistle grabbed a bucket and threw it in the face of the approaching man to extinguish the smouldering stove in his mouth before the fire spread to the person in danger.

It didn't take long for a chaotic mess to develop, with everyone running around in dripping wet clothes, always on the alert to throw a bucket of water in the face of the nearest person in order to prevent the fire in his mouth from spreading to other parts of his body.

That was enough for Uhlenspiegel, his earnings had been tolerable and on top of that he had had his fun. He departed after his work was done, leaving Schilda, its citizens, the buckets filled with water and the stoves stuck in their mouths to themselves to recover from the rascal's exertions.

5.
Fairytale everyday life

*W*hen Uhlenspiegel realized once again that his own purse was as empty as the mayor's, he turned to the good citizens of Schilda to remedy his plight. He put on a terribly suffering face, forced his small round belly into a corset so that it soon threatened to come out at the back, thought of some unpleasant people to drive worry lines into his face and set off.

A few days later, he was standing in the market square of Schilda, standing and standing and just looking up at the sky. It was a short while before the first citizen of Schilda stopped to observe his strange behavior. Uhlenspiegel paid no attention to him but continued to gaze intently into the air. More and more curious people gathered around him and finally he was able to avert his eyes from the heavenly sight to occupy himself with earthly things.

Why are you staring at me and bothering me while I'm earning money? he said peevishly. Do you think I would just stare at the clouds out of sheer amusement, when all they do is pour rain on you as soon as they are tired of carrying their burden or looking at you?

Quiet guilt arose in the citizens of Schilda, for they had disturbed a venerable guest from looking at their sky, who had immediately made it rain on them with guilt, and on top of that they had disturbed Uhlenspiegel from earning money that he could then conveniently spend on them. So Uhlenspiegel went one step further in his plan and told the story of the Star Money Child, it had never been told in a more heart-rending way and soon the tears flowed as if all the floodgates of heaven had been opened.

Why do you grieve over this report? asked Uhlenspiegel with the holy glow of pity, have you not heard that the child was showered with golden coins at the end and that at the even later end there was no one on earth who could match her in wealth?

Slowly the tears drained away and the citizens of Schilda became aware of the light in the story. If you could be this star money child, you would gladly wade through hardship for a short time to end up better off than everyone else.

You are right, cried Uhlenspiegel, for you need not think that I cannot read your thoughts. Even with those whose hair is not yet so thinned that it is easy to look inside their heads. You must, you must first create hardship for yourselves so that in the end the coins will fall on your heads.

That sounded obvious, but how could the citizens of Schilda create their own hardship?

You have far too much in your houses, bring it here tomorrow, I'll take the trouble to take care of all this unnecessary garbage. And bring all the money you have hidden in your socks, under your pillows and elsewhere in holes, or have you heard that the star money child had even a single penny?

The next day, what Uhlenspiegel had suggested happened and it took him several days to get rid of all these trivialities. In the meantime, he told the citizens of Schilda to be patient, as no gold coins were falling from the sky, it could only mean that their need was not yet great enough and that he or they should think about how to remedy it.

Another day later, when everyone had gathered in the marketplace, they looked at Uhlenspiegel anxiously.

Had they forgotten how thin the little arms of the star money child were? And why hadn't they thought of bringing their secret treasures from the larders here themselves, not forgetting all the fragrant bacon and ham, the smoked sausage and the sweet wine, instead of secretly filling their bellies?

Thus, it happened and Uhlenspiegel was able to fill his belly in secret. But this secrecy had to take place during the day, for the citizens of Schilda slept full of self-denial when the bright sun shone in order to stand under the sky at night, waiting for the gold coins to rain down.

The year was well advanced, and the first snow had fallen on the fields when the citizens of Schilda once again stood around Uhlenspiegel in the market square. Uhlenspiegel was visibly angry. All the trouble he had gone to with them, while their stubborn comfort still prevented the heavens from making gold coins snow down.

The child had worn just a thin shirt, despite the snow and frost, her arms and legs trembling, which, by the way, and therefore they didn't need to worry too much, signified – he meant the trembling – that the body produced its own warmth to ward off frost and ice.

Soon afterwards, a considerable pile of clothes was piled up in the middle of the market square and Uhlenspiegel had trouble choosing the most splendid pieces. Among the citizens of Schilda, however, there was a gnashing of teeth and a clamor that rivaled the frost's ringing.

When the shower of gold coins still failed to materialize, Uhlenspiegel stood in the marketplace one last time. His pockets were overflowing with money, his belly was filled to overflowing with the finest delicacies and everything, even his handsome doublet, was covered in the finest fabric and the thickest fur coats.

I am tired of having to explain the story to you again and again. But since I see the trouble you have got yourselves into, but not yet deep enough to get the good end, I will undertake to tell you the last secret of your lack of hardship. He spared them the part of the story about the star money child being half-orphaned, not wanting to be responsible for serious disputes in order to get hold of this misery too.

Did you hear that the star money child had a warm home, sat comfortably in front of a smoking stove and enjoyed the warm fire? You must do away with your houses, said Uhlenspiegel sadly, but for your sake I will ask the night sky to understand that all you have to do is knock out the windows and doors and it will still be ready to pour down its gold coins.

Uhlenspiegel even offered to help with this work and was the first to carry out the peculiar craft. It seemed to give him particular satisfaction to carry out such work on the town hall and the mayor's house. Everywhere the windows rattled and the wooden doors burst open so that sparks flew around your ears. As night fell, it was fortunate that a comet passed over Schilda that day and a shower of shooting stars fell.

Keep on hitting hard, shouted Uhlenspiegel into the din, look, the evening sky is preparing to give you the good end, so hurry into the forest to pick up the gold coins.

What happened next is not recorded, only that Uhlenspiegel had a lot to do in the time that followed to enjoy the wealth he had acquired and that he could hardly keep up with spending all the money. Yes, he even had to change his clothes every hour to put on all the precious cloth garments and so, much to the chagrin of the people of Schilda, he spent the next few years alternating between eating, spending money and changing clothes from morning to night.

6.
Dry run

*T*he land had dried up to the last drop, as the sun had taken it upon itself to shine down on Schilda incessantly, by day and even by night. Not so much to bring enlightenment where such inspirations were not needed or seemed hopeless, but rather the yellow orb seemed to enjoy watching the strange goings-on in that place. The fields were as dry as straw, which usually only floated at a reasonable height above the ground. Cows expressed their displeasure so loudly that it was impossible to hold a council meeting during the day, sleep soundly at a meeting or indulge in sweet dreams at night.

Advice was needed, advice and water, water advice, so to speak, which perhaps every councilor would pour into themselves beforehand. So, they collected, not the water, but the council, and held a council meeting.

The citizens of Schilda now benefited from having a pious hermit in their ranks, even if not in their midst, as he usually lived in caves. Because he had a long beard and for washing, and therefore also for waxing beards (washing ---> waxing, in a petulant mood some letters had switched their place in life, washing had appeared to him in the form of solidified wax and therefore, but also because of the shortage of water, he had decided to no longer wash his beard but to wax it without further ado), whatever the case, because a few drops of water were needed in any case, he seemed the right man to come up with a fitting solution.

He rose to his feet and began to talk slowly about people from distant times who wanted to build a high tower to see what was going on in the sky.

Nobody yet understood what the solution to the story was until the pious hermit explained meaningfully that the water came from the clouds and that all you had to do was build a clock tower and then get a good number of clouds to fly into the tower and climb down to earth. You could make the inside of the tower cozy, with everything that clouds liked, feathers, sheep, wind, withered leaves and much more.

Fortunately, before they started to turn the plan into practice, one of their brightest had the idea of asking what had happened to those people and, in general, what it was like in heaven and whether there was enough water there. Because that much seemed clear, if they didn't get any water and heaven had enough of it, they would leave the place without further ado and build a new heavenly Schilda above the clouds.

When they heard about the confusion of languages, which could not have come about in any other way than that everyone had grown different knots in their tongues and, anyway, how were they supposed to drink the water that was then available with knots in their tongues, it was unanimously decided to send the hermit back from where he had come from and to send a new plan.

However, this was not enough to find a solution. The fields became even drier, the cows bellowed louder than before and the make-up applied to the human faces peeled off like loose plaster, as the skin looked more and more like a ripped-open desert.

However, it soon occurred to them that the solution was in the cows. They would be locked up in the town hall so that they didn't suck the last of the water from the meadows. People would also no longer have to put up with their loud bellowing. Perhaps they could also be persuaded to provide water instead of milk, if not voluntarily, they would just have to find suitable fodder.

And, this was the most important part of the cow solution, someone had remembered that small clouds came out of the cows' mouths, especially in the morning. Occasionally from the rear end too, but these could be dispensed with if the front ones were plentiful enough. All you had to do was catch the cow clouds, which incidentally did not require a tower reaching up to the sky, and then squeeze them out like a wet sponge.

That's what happened. The officials left the town hall and (other) cattle were locked in the offices. Each cow had a tightly woven linen sack tied around its head to catch the little clouds, but this did nothing to calm its bellowing. Every hour on the hour, they checked to see how much water had collected in the sack. The result was devastating and soon the cows were suspected of drinking the precious water from the mouth sacks themselves. A rope was therefore tied around their necks, just tight enough to allow air to pass through, but no more water to flow in.

That didn't help either. The next morning, however, the tranquil little town realized that the clever idea had at least stopped the cows bellowing, even if no water had been brought to light. When they entered the town hall to find out the cause of the strange silence, they found all the cattle lying dead as a doornail on the floor. The neck ropes had done a great job.

It did not occur to them to try the same experiment with the original inhabitants of the town hall, as they had never seen any of these creatures so early in the morning, nor had they ever seen small clouds of water coming out of their mouths, nor had they ever seen them doing such strenuous work that they could have tried to extract water in this way.

So, they turned to far-reaching connections and well-established contacts with a small town on the other side of the world, where it rained so much that it regularly turned into a bathtub. An envoy was assembled to visit this remote place;

a contract was made for them to buy a good portion of rain, and one of them would be able to figure out how to transport it on the long journey. And in return, the legation could offer the inexhaustible knowledge of Schilda, which could solve any problem on this earth.

Moreover, by being willing to bring some of the rain to Schilda, the problem of the large bathtub for the place on the other side of the world would disappear as if by magic, which meant nothing other than dry air.

What's more, it would not have been the first time that the world had been shown that, even with their own little Schilda heads, they were capable of solving the world's impending problems, possibly caused by freak weather conditions, without having to consult that unfortunate fellow Uhlenspiegel, who had often managed to turn a small problem into far more than a thousand larger ones despite his best intentions.

7.
The black smoldering rose

*I*t was around the time that spring turned to summer. Three years ago, a strange visitor came through Schilda. At that time and later, it was impossible to find out whether his appearance was accidental or intentional, but one day he was simply there.

He had nothing special to show, was dressed like everyone else, neither remarkably short nor tall, just an average person. Except for one small thing that he carried in his hands. A flower. A rose. A black rose. No one had ever seen anything like it in Schilda, so it was only logical that he soon became the center of attention in the village.

At first, he didn't seem to care much, but when he realized that there was a considerable amount of business to be done in this place with a black rose, his interest skyrocketed. Every citizen in Schilda owned a garden and proved to be extremely thorough when it came to flora.

Without further ado, a large gathering was convened in the market square to hear the explanation for the miracle and soon to see black roses in their own gardens.

The visitor had put on a white coat, which made him look even more impressive. He explained that he was a doctor of plants; just like humans and livestock, these beings also need expert help. And one day, yes, you heard right, a black rose had come to him. He had not seen it with his own eyes, but it could only have come running along, just as people and animals used to come along on their feet. When it arrived, however, it was so exhausted from the long journey that it could no longer move, stood rooted to the spot and even lacked the strength to speak.

Of course, at first he had thought that the black color was simply due to dirt, that it could just be rinsed off. This soon turned out to be a misconception, and it had taken him half his life to find out, through elaborate experiments, what this miracle was based on.

At these words, he pulled a round glass disk out of his pocket and held it up meaningfully. Then he told some of the bystanders to look through the glass into the sun. Their mouths flew open like wide barn doors.

The sun is a terrible deceiver, said the man, everyone thinks it paints the world yellow, but in reality, it hides all sorts of other colors in its rays to play tricks with. How else can you explain the fact that you sometimes turn red or brown when the sun has been shining on your head for too long? He only knew of one country where people were yellow from the sun. On the other side of the world, they were red because they always stood in the sunrise to enjoy the sight of the red color. He had even heard of green people, whether on this globe or somewhere else, but he couldn't remember.

The same applies to the plants. Why are all the flowers as colorful as a patchwork quilt? Because they get different amounts of the sun's colors. And these are everywhere, even in the water, which undoubtedly explains the bright colors of the fish. There is only one color that the sun does not know. Black. Otherwise, it would also shine at night. And does it shine at night? Certainly not, as anyone can confirm.

It would also be easy to grow black roses. If you could get them to not close their flowers at night. Then the black color of the night could soak into the blossoms, voila, the next day you would have a black rose. However, even he couldn't figure out how to get a rose not to close its flowers at night. And since he himself closes his eyes at night, perhaps to save his beautiful blue eyes from the black of the night, the same right must be granted to roses.

Therefore, and he is not only the first but also the only person to have discovered this, there is no other way to preserve a black rose than to let it grow upside down in the ground.

It is dark in the earth, as all the dead could confirm if they were still able to speak. The rose cannot keep its blossoms closed indefinitely, just as a person immersed in water cannot keep his mouth closed indefinitely. He would open it once, even if he knew he was sucking in water and not air. And it would be the same with roses, at first they would stubbornly refuse to open their blossoms, like someone who has been under water for an hour; and at some point they would not be able to avoid it and at the same moment the black darkness of the earth would creep into the blossom and you would have the desired success. All you have to do is pull them upside down out of the ground by the roots. Incidentally, no one needs to be afraid of rose thorns, as they cannot be seen in the black earth, so they cannot be able to feel or prick.

That was convincing. It hardly deserves mentioning that, despite the convincing speech, interposed questions were asked, such as why a black tent was not placed over the rose to trick it. The foreign visitor called the questioner a fool, asking if he didn't know that the sun's rays wouldn't be taken by surprise by such a pathetic idea, that they were everywhere, even if you weren't aware of them. Just not in the earth.

Nevertheless, he wanted to try to take a positive suggestion from this actually impertinent question and therefore advised burying the roses deep enough, as his research had not extended to the point of how deeply the sun's rays are able to penetrate the ground. He himself had achieved the best success with a planting depth of seven meters, which is little compared to the toil of digging a well, and what does the insignificant water, which is available everywhere, represent compared to the rarity of a black rose?

There was still one small thing to consider. Of course, the rose could remember the position of the sun and get the idea of growing back up out of the hole. The first few times this mishap also happened to him. This could only be prevented by lighting a proper fire under the planting hole at an even greater depth to trick the rose into thinking it was in the sun and encourage it to grow further into the depths, towards the supposed sun.

Needless to say, soon afterwards there were no more roses to be seen in Schilda, but plenty of smoking holes in the ground, as if the tranquil town had suddenly migrated to a seething volcanic island.

The strange visitor, in whom the name Uhlenspiegel may have been hidden, had long since moved on. He had had his only epiphany during a boring school lesson when he placed a rose, which he wanted to put on his neighbor's chair for the sake of the thorns, in the black inkwell, where he had forgotten it for a while to enhance the effect of his plan.

This also proved that even boring school lessons have their positive sides, as he decided to leave school behind from then on and travel the world with his unexpected discovery, knowing full well that he would come across plenty of people on earth who had made even less progress with their learning than he had and who would marvel at his discovery with their mouths wide open. This was also the case in the tranquil town of Schilda, where not only the chimneys but also the ground smoked at every conceivable corner.

8.

House-stacked time

One of the three citizens of Schilda who had undertaken to go out into the wide world and who had managed or found it worthwhile to return to Schilda was a man with white gray hair. His unexpected return was like an earthquake that triggered an almost endless chain of celebrations. At the end of this orgy of festivities, it was decided to take advantage of his return and what he had experienced. One had to move with the times, otherwise time would suddenly run out, which meant that all the clocks would stop running because time had run out, and if there was no more time in Schilda, everyone would inevitably die. Because how could anyone live on without time?

So, this return was a gift of fate, not only of great interest because of the news, but also of the utmost importance. Therefore, the far-traveled man was to tell one piece of news every day and everyone would make an effort to do the same, otherwise time would run out.

All the citizens of Schilda were gathered, as everyone felt that not only the existence of their town, but even their own lives depended on the important message.

The first thing he had to tell, the well-traveled man began, was about cities where people lived on top of each other. Stacked on top of each other so that the top of the houses disappeared into the clouds. He had also heard that prices at the very top were also at the very top, presumably because the air was the cleanest there, the sun the closest, the view the widest, in short, life was the most beautiful and the sky, where everyone wanted to go, was the densest.

At these words, he fell to the ground, dead as a doornail. The powerful memory must have been too great for him. On the one hand, the others were glad not to have exposed themselves to such life-threatening impressions, but on the other hand, they had to act quickly to put the news into practice, so that at least they would have something new to keep time from running away from their Schilda.

The very next day, work began on building the house that would grow into the clouds. It took three weeks to erect the first house. It was beautiful to look at, with white windows, red tiles and a pointed thatched roof. But this is where the real problem began.

How could you build a second house on a pointed roof without it falling down? Perhaps the second house should be built upside down so that the peak would lie on top of the peak and a good layer of glue should be applied in between. However, this would mean that the inhabitants of the second house would have to move upside down in their dwelling, which seemed rather complicated for certain activities such as eating and perhaps also for the opposite of eating.

So, without further ado, a platform was erected above the first house, supported by the thickest beams that could be found, and the second house was built on top of it. They continued in this way until five houses stood on top of each other. An impressive pyramid had been created, five houses built on top of each other. But time had to be impressed in order to persuade them not to run away from this unique innovation.

The fact that nobody knew how to get into the upper houses was a minor problem for the time being, as they had forgotten to install any steps, ladders, stairs or openings in the platforms. Nevertheless, the problem had to be solved in the long term. Mother Nature alone was able to do this. Trees were planted on the left and right, on the left side a variety that grew slowly, but in time reached the clouds so that you could climb over them to the top house.

On the right-hand side, trees were planted that grew so quickly that you could watch them, so all you had to do was sit on one of their crowns and wait until it had reached the desired height, enjoying the beautiful view, knowing that you would soon be able to look down majestically from a clear height on to the heads that had become bald from all the thinking.

9.
A strange unfortunate chain of events

*U*hlenspiegel realized that he had not paid his respects to the citizens of Schilda for some time. The sky was gray, the chilly air overflowing with rain, but the dreary mood was not to deter him from his plans.

First of all, he had to find a suitable way to make the journey. He thought of an old sledge, and as he thought about it, the old wooden rocking horse came to mind. So, he tied the wooden horse to the sledge, equipped himself with some round logs and, as you can easily imagine, began his journey. He benefited from the fact that the terrain was somewhat sloping. Laying the round logs in front of the sledge, he slid forward bit by bit, jumping off his high horse to collect his mobile track and throw it, the round logs, back in front of the sledge. He soon had the idea of connecting each piece of wood with a rope. In this way, he only had to wait until the sledge had whizzed over the wood and rope to reach back and fling the whole thing back in front of his vehicle with an elegant swing. Over time, he became so practiced that he reached a speed that even the birds in the air were unable to keep up with.

In the aforementioned manner, he rushed towards the small town of Schilda. The citizens of Schilda were quite astonished when they saw the strange vehicle. It was not enough for Uhlenspiegel to simply move the vehicle, he now had to bring it to a halt. He only managed to do this by smashing his vehicle through the outer wall of the town hall and coming to a halt right on the mayor's desk.

Despite the shock, the first thing Uhlenspiegel had to do was to take a white sheet of paper and a quill pen and write the citizens of Schilda a proper bill:

For breaking out a window, I take the liberty of charging the people of Schilda 100 thalers. I will send the amount for the repair of my sledge separately. My horse, however, takes the liberty of submitting an invoice for 100 boxes of apples and 50 bales of straw, payable in cash if you are so kind.

Signed: Uhlenspiegel

The citizens were happy to pay, as they no longer had to bring light into the town hall to make their mayor's broad, sweaty red head shine. But they paid the other in kind, as they wanted to see a wooden horse lying down on straw and eating the juicy red apples that would come out the other end in the same size and shape, only in a different color. How else would it be able to devour the enormous amount of fruit?

Uhlenspiegel told the citizens of Schilda to gather in the market square the next day. A new era had dawned, and he had taken the trouble to carry progress to the remotest corners of the earth. It is hard to guess what he told the citizens of Schilda the next day. Soon all the citizens of Schilda were busy chopping down all the trees in the visible area and splitting them into arm-length pieces.

Sledges were made from the branches and when the work was done to Uhlenspiegel's complete satisfaction, the rogue told them to gather again on the market square.

You can rest your feet, said Uhlenspiegel. The time for you to touch the dirty earth where your cows do their business with these precious objects is over. But progress has not yet fully arrived. Rather, we are not spared from dividing the citizenry into two halves. I propose dividing it according to sex, for what else distinguishes you more than this triviality?

However, Uhlenspiegel continued, the roles should be switched so that everything is in order. On odd-numbered days, it would be the women's turn.

But what roles, what classes was Uhlenspiegel actually talking about? He meant nothing other than that one role was to sit on the sledge, whatever the weather. The other role was to run alongside and throw the arm-length pieces of tree in front of the sledge so that it made good progress. Progress, however, consisted of doing nothing, at least on even or odd days, depending on which gender you belonged to.

The fact that it meant all the more work the next day, because the pieces of tree weighed a fair amount, was to be accepted. Every step forward also entailed minor inconvenience.

Uhlenspiegel watched the strange spectacle for a week and decided to let the citizens of Schilda take part in another piece of progress. There were enough pieces of tree to line all the paths.

So there was no longer any need for the effort of running alongside. He, Uhlenspiegel, had clairvoyant abilities and time had allowed him to look into the future. There he saw that in the not too distant future, people would only be able to be transported anywhere on rolling carts.

The fact that they no longer had any trees was of little concern to the citizens of Schilda. This would allow them to recognize the robbers sneaking through the forest in good time. And on top of that, hunting was much easier, because where would wild boar, hares and hedgehogs hide now? In the wake of progress come many small conveniences, which greatly increased the importance of Uhlenspiegel's invention and consequently his reward.

After a few days, when all the tree parts lay like a wedged together ball of wool on the marketplace and paths, Uhlenspiegel thought it was time to leave the tranquil place. He had all the sledges tied together in a huge chain. As the tracks had to be repaired first, the sledges would not be needed for the next few days. Then he had them loaded up. The rest of the bales of straw and apples that his wooden horse hadn't eaten and the appropriate remuneration for his work were left for him. Together in such numbers that the 100 sledges were not enough to carry everything away.

But how could he set the strange chain of sledges in motion?

Some of you must pull me! cried Uhlenspiegel. After all, it is your belongings that I have to take away. But let's take advantage of having divided you into two halves. The men should take on the hard work of preparing the roads, while the women should pull him home.

Even the citizens of Schilda understood that. But perhaps they were just glad to be rid of this strange fellow, even if it cost them their possessions and, for a while, their wives. It was summer and the heat was baking on people's heads. Uhlenspiegel, however, sat on his sledge, enjoying the beautiful sight – not so much the landscape, all the trees had disappeared – but more the backs of all the women of Schilda and feasted on the precious food he had loaded, jumping from one sledge to the next from time to time like a flea gone wild and occasionally urging his two-legged horses to hurry.

10.
Make one out of two (by yourself)

*T*he next time Uhlenspiegel came to Schilda, he immediately noticed that the town was up to its neck in water. As a precious commodity, however, it would not even be up to the soles of their feet, for the city coffers of Schilda were empty, empty like the enormous black holes that circled through the distant sky, waiting for unsuspecting victims. As Uhlenspiegel was well versed in money matters, even though he had never received any instruction or training in them, he offered to help the citizens of Schilda out of their predicament.

Your city treasury is like a wine barrel, explained Uhlenspiegel. On one side you pour in new wine, on the other you take it away again. How is the barrel supposed to fill up?

We can enlarge the inlet considerably, Uhlenspiegel continued. He didn't feel like blocking the outlet. In a figurative sense, it would also stop the drinking of wine; he couldn't expect anyone to stop drinking wine, not himself and not the citizens of Schilda.

You need a capable tax collector, continued Uhlenspiegel. I have experience with such things. What could be more natural than to let me do this work?

That made sense and Uhlenspiegel was appointed Schilda's tax collector. He needed to gain a little more trust for himself. So he decided to set an example. He reached for his pouch and poured all his possessions out on to the table.

You take four parts of all this in taxes, said Uhlenspiegel. How are you supposed to fill your tax coffers? You must take seven parts. Soon your situation will be different.

In front of the astonished eyes of the citizens of Schilda, Uhlenspiegel took seven parts from his own property and put them in the city coffers. The fact that it was his task to manage the city treasury, which for good reason also involved supervision, should not be mentioned here.

And why do you only collect taxes once a year? Doesn't the sun rise every day? Do as the sun does, soon your city coffers will be shining brightly like the sun.

In this way, Uhlenspiegel collected the taxes, day after day, each day seven parts of what was left over from the previous day. As he was so busy, he never got around to collecting taxes from himself. His time was just enough to get back the seven parts he had taken from himself at the beginning. He had also negotiated his reward with the mayor to keep all the taxes he collected on odd-numbered days as payment. The taxes collected on even days went to the city coffers.

As one is an odd number, the first tax rate was always levied on an odd numbered day. Nevertheless, the tax coffers slowly began to fill up. The citizens were proud of this, forgetting their own poverty, the pride in their city becoming richer made them forget their poverty.

When the pile of revenue could no longer be increased and the citizens of Schilda resembled an image of the seven lean cows that the young man Joseph had seen in a dream many 100 years ago, Uhlenspiegel decided to turn his attention to the expenditure side.

Citizens of Schilda, he said, we have gone to great lengths to squeeze taxes out of ourselves in order to fill our beloved city coffers again. Why bother, because we throw everything out of the window again with open hands, even if your town hall, which has no windows, still throws the most out on to the street. I am ashamed to have to choose these drastic words.

Why put all your money somewhere for your civil servants, who do nothing else for half the day but sit on their backsides, which can easily compete with the rear ends of your oxen regarding the sitting and fattening. Who pays you for sitting around and for the nasty concoction of the many wickednesses with which you maltreat and torment each other? We can safely abolish half of the whole, there is still a whole part left to work.

The citizens of Schilda nodded in unison. Uhlenspiegel continued on the wave of their approval:

We will merge. The magic word is: joining forces. Everything will be easier and cheaper. First of all, we'll only keep half a policeman and half a judge. How is that supposed to work? you will think. We can't go about splitting the policeman and the judge in half from top to bottom and putting one half of each together to make something new.

It's easier than you think, because the solution is in me. So never forget how good you had it because I took on so much and tell your children about it so that I live on in their minds, even if my old shell is already resting under your cows grazing the lush grass.

I hereby decree that we dismiss your policeman and your judge. They are to help in the pasture so that you can sit in front of a bigger butter mountain in winter than ever before. But half of me will be your new policeman and the other half your judge. But decide for yourself whether my right or left half should be a policeman and whether my left or right half should be a judge. But you only pay me the salary for one person. You see what a fine saving you'll make.

Everyone nodded. The citizens of Schilda understood, and they didn't understand, they had no idea what the amalgamation would mean for them. The cows hardly gave any milk – under the strange methods of a retired judge and policeman, they refused to continue producing the white liquid, as they were tired of working under duress and the constant daily weighing up of how much milk they were allowed to produce each day.

They even refused to eat any more, voluntarily ceasing their favorite activity, so that the citizens of Schilda felt compelled to move the former judge and the former policeman to a remote barren island where they could do no more harm.

Uhlenspiegel, however, carried out his work with such zeal that one could be forgiven for thinking that his person had been chained together from ten officious judges and just as many zealous policemen. He arrested, imprisoned, sentenced, pardoned, sentenced again, revoked promised pardons, so that it would have been a pleasure for the old judge to see this activity.

The miraculous solution had indeed been found in the collaboration. The expenses were halved and Uhlenspiegel's one half got on so well with the other that not a few times the gendarme in him became active even before his legal half had given the order. Since Uhlenspiegel, by virtue of his person and his office, forbade children from crying from the first day of their lives, women from chatting loudly and all men from blowing their noses, spitting and burping without restraint, a heavenly peace soon returned to Schilda.

He had a huge statue of himself erected on the market square, with two faces like Siamese twins, one looking down on Schilda with suspicious eyes, the other cast in an icy expression that made some good citizens of Schilda shiver even in summer as they passed by the awe-inspiring monument.

Of course, this was not allowed to happen free of charge. Anyone walking past the monument had to pay the equivalent of one thaler into the offering box, which Uhlenspiegel had brought from the church to the market square. And Uhlenspiegel issued regulations, compliance with which inevitably meant that every being in Schilda had to pass by his monument at least once a day.

Over time, Uhlenspiegel grew weary of his own capriciousness. He was overcome by the suspicious feeling that the citizens of Schilda secretly did not show him the slightest amount of the respect and reverence he deserved for his dignity, work and selfless sacrifice. He therefore had the stone monument removed and half of it rebuilt in a quiet forest clearing and the other half on the top of the highest mountain. At the former site on the market square, he had a huge, deep hole dug so that the citizens of Schilda would be reminded for all time of the great loss they had suffered. For he disappeared the next day, along with his office and dignity, his sacrificial box and even his taxes, which he had first extorted from himself, albeit only temporarily, with unparalleled self-mortification.

11.
Sweet post-Christmas decree

*T*he Christmas festivities had come to an end, more extravagant than in previous years, more Christmas trees had been cut, more Christmas angels had arrived and taken off again from the market square, and the many reindeer from Santa Claus's countless herd had disappeared into the surrounding woods.

No-one had thought of the consequences, and they only became apparent when the baker could no longer perform half of his trade of baking cakes. There was a lack of sugar everywhere, every sweet white grain had fallen victim to the extravagant Christmas feast.

Now sweet advice was at a premium, because what is life, especially in the afternoon or on Sundays, without cake? Perhaps the solution lay in another problem. Because too little salt had been used in baking in winter, just like in this sweet season, and so the salt stores were in danger of bursting at the seams. Now it's only a short distance from salt to sugar, as anyone who has inadvertently messed with the salt barrel rather than the cook in the kitchen knows. It was impossible to tell the difference between the two in terms of appearance, and didn't it take the kind of trained taste that was only found in Schilda to distinguish between the two? Perhaps, for the sake of simplicity, no distinction was made out there in the big wide world.

We've become too sophisticated, thought the mayor, who else could afford to tell the difference between salt and sugar. But the wheel of history could not be turned back, he had to live with the fact that his village consisted only of gourmets. However, it explained the high price of sugar that the foreign traders demanded. It could not be otherwise than that they had to go to unbearable lengths, like a whitewashed Cinderella, to pick out the sweet grains of sugar from the large salt mountains.

This consideration led him dangerously far, namely to cancel the next Christmas, the city coffers were empty anyway and the sweet vice must finally come to an end.

However, he paused here to deal with the current problem first. He knew that the village beekeeper had a considerable supply of honey, which he spread on the flowers every spring to make the bees' work easier. They must be about the same age as him, 80 years, as they came every year, and at their burdensome age, didn't they deserve to toil a little less?

If the beekeeper dispensed with this procedure once, every grain of salt could be brushed with honey. It would have to be someone else's business if it didn't taste like honey afterwards, or at least sweet. The color seemed to be a minor problem; people had heard of brown sugar, the dark color because it was transported in brown tubes, so they would simply declare the salted honey to be brown sugar.

The endeavor failed, however, as no brush could be found that was fine enough to paste a grain of salt with honey.

So the mayor decided to issue a decree that, with immediate effect, salt was to be declared sugar. Everyone had to remember the former taste when eating it and it was forbidden under threat of punishment not to remember the past sweet taste or to make an ugly face while eating.

However, as he was a caring father and knew himself to be the lord over clever subjects, he was gracious enough to add an explanation to the occasion.

This time the sugar had been brought by a different route, which was dangerous and inadequate. However, no expense or effort had been spared for the people of the village. The only problem was that the sugar had been shaken so vigorously during the brave journey that the husk had flaked off every grain and it therefore tasted slightly different this year. An effort was made to pick up the chipped sweet shells and put the white grains back in. However, this was not an insignificant amount of work, as each kernel had to be assigned the right shell, otherwise it would have had to be trimmed to the exact size beforehand. But they were hopeful, just as women are sometimes hopeful, that they would be finished with the work by next Christmas.

Until then, everyone would be pleased to live with the substitute and remember the good times and the good ingredients that they used to have and which, as true as he was mayor, would soon return to their place in a positive sense after a joint effort.

And thus, it happened, not as far as the good times were concerned, because these cannot be so easily ordered by a mayor, but rather with the prescribed substitute.

12.
Death without end

*O*ne morning, as Uhlenspiegel stood in front of the mirror, quite grumpy and hung over from a night's drinking, a strange thought occurred to him, certainly not for the first time, but perhaps for the last. All the years had taken their toll on him, leaving huge valleys in his face, gnawing at his bones like cheese full of holes, turning his veins into bulging wineskins in which the blood sloshed back and forth and only made it to the highest point, his head, with difficulty.

Everything in life needs practice, thought Uhlenspiegel, in order to succeed perfectly. He thought of the showmen he had met at the fair who had taught him the secrets of the stage. All you need is a short, effective beginning and an equally short, surprising ending; it's not worth spending too much effort on the laborious, long middle of the play. And an effective ending is useful to stick in the minds of the spectators.

So, these showmen spent most of their lives practicing the strangest contortions with which they wanted to appear before the applauding audience at the end of their performances.

Even the end has to be practiced, Uhlenspiegel said to himself, perhaps more than anything else. Wasn't the whole of existence nothing more than a big stage where people laughed, gawked, lied and cheated to distract their minds from the banal adversities of everyday life? And anyway, who knew where the journey would take you after your appearance on this stage, perhaps you would be placed in a new position in that other world that came after death, which depended only on how you left this miserable earthen stage. Uhlenspiegel didn't feel like dying yet, but it couldn't do any harm to rehearse for this event so that he would be prepared to do his work when Grim Reaper appeared at the door.

Remorseful, he set off, and what better place than Schilda. The citizens of Schilda knew how to deal with death. The houses had simply been built without windows and doors so that death could not enter. And if he did manage to get in, it was as dark as a belly cavity inside, so he couldn't find anyone and would end up perishing miserably in the dark himself.

The next morning he reached Schilda, the weather was splendidly prepared for this strange occasion, black chains of rain everywhere, from which tears rained incessantly.

I have sometimes played nasty tricks on you, Uhlenspiegel began his speech in the market square, where quite a few citizens of Schilda had stopped in curious anticipation of what this strange fellow had to say this time.

Death is gnawing at me, Uhlenspiegel continued, tears in his eyes competing with the rain clouds, it is gnawing everywhere, at my bones, my hands, my eyes, even the ends of my hair, where it has already greedily sucked out the wonderful wine-red color and left behind a nasty gray.

I must confess that it is also gnawing at my conscience, continued Uhlenspiegel in a voice choked with tears, I will have to take all the evil deeds I have committed to my grave.

He already had to apologize to the cemetery graves diggers for having to dig a much bigger grave for all these things, all the bad deeds, a burden so heavy that you have to worry whether the coffin won't simply break through the earth because of the unbearable weight and reappear at the other end of the globe.

Nevertheless, I have decided to repent and stand up straight for everything, or rather lie down straight, as it is generally known that one lies down when it is time to start the journey underground. As a sign of my repentance, I will lie down in the grave before death has finished its terrible work. Heaven, perhaps it will remember my repentance at this sight, so that I don't have to go straight to the purgatory of hell.

The citizens of Schilda were astonished. Some reverently expressed their respect for this kind of penitence, which had never reached their ears before.

All kinds of requests were made as to how to negotiate with Death so that he would let go of Uhlenspiegel. They, the citizens of Schilda, were prepared to sacrifice their most beautiful cow, which Death could nibble on as he pleased if he refrained from playing such bad jokes on the poor penitent sinner.

I thank you, said Uhlenspiegel graciously, but I cannot agree to such an exchange. Every morning you will think of your faithful, expensive cow, of her miraculous milk, when you have to drink the stinking white soup of a goat instead. And then there's the feast! When a tough piece of meat gets stuck in your throat, the last image that will appear to you will be your dear cow, her tender flanks that would have melted like honey on your palate. Incidentally, I have already prepared everything.

He had also come to an agreement with Death. Together they had chosen a magnificent oak tree where he, Uhlenspiegel, would have his final resting place.

You will hear my eternal tears if you pass by this tree when the wind rustles the leaves and in this way you will never forget that I have visited your home many a time, for the benefit of both of us.

Uhlenspiegel knew that the mayor of Schilda had traveled far and wide through wondrous lands for his official duties. These journeys had eaten large holes in the tax coffers, but the citizens of Schilda had a man of the world at their disposal who knew how to tell the most incredible stories in wine-filled hours. And Uhlenspiegel knew very well that the rotund figure of the mayor, like a tireless perpetual motion machine, was constantly pushing to become the center of attention.

On one of my journeys, the mayor began his unctuous speech, and now you can see once again how useful it is for you that I have taken on these arduous journeys, on one of these journeys I met a people who had built a huge mountain of stone, pointed and high, to bury a dead man. These people knew about the mysterious journey that every dead person had to make and so they put all sorts of gifts in the grave to make the journey more pleasant for the deceased: the best wine, bread and sausage for a few weeks, because the journey would definitely take that long, precious garments for the festivities that had to be celebrated on the way and gold to appease the disgruntled monsters that one encounters on such a journey.

And twice as much of each, Uhlenspiegel interjected, don't forget that I'm not dead yet when you put me in the grave. So I need an extra portion of everything for the last days of my life.

Why shouldn't he nibble on something while death nibbled on him?

Twice as much of each, the mayor faltered, and he realized that the memory of that journey had come at a bad time. He was already thinking hard about how to get out of this unscathed, thick beads of sweat running down his bulging cheeks, and Uhlenspiegel realized that he had to add something quickly to ensure his own death.

I understand that it makes you sweat with fear, thinking of my difficult path, he called out to the mayor. And perhaps your nobleness makes you think of how to spare me all this. But remember: the spirit is willing and the flesh is weak. If you let me get away alive, it may happen that remorse will leave my spirit and the flesh of my fingers will begin to twitch again to play another trick on you.

He didn't need to elaborate any further, he didn't need to list any of the many evil deeds to make it clear to the citizens of Schilda that they had gotten themselves into an expensive affair, but that they would be able to live in unclouded peace for all time.

It was agreed that by the next day, all the necessary traveling utensils, bacon, cheese, wine, silk robes, gold coins and the like should be brought to the oak tree to be placed in the grave that Uhlenspiegel, not wanting to cause them any additional trouble, had already dug, so that everything could be placed in the grave together with Uhlenspiegel.

And so it was done. As was customary, a solemn ceremony was held. The mayor appointed himself the main speaker and showered the deceased with courtesies. He was to be praised for his wealth of ideas, his most polite manners, he had broadened the horizons of the citizens of Schilda enormously, had torn down the old to make room for the new and, what was particularly important to remember at such an hour, had shown them the futility of wealth by ridding them of this superfluous trinket more than once. Even now, in the hour of his greatest need, he had offered to take this accumulated mammon into the pit as a burden.

When the gracious speech had ended, Uhlenspiegel climbed into the coffin without a word of farewell, ordered the lid to be closed and, as had been agreed, earth to be thrown over the whole thing. Under no circumstances should anyone, fueled by a curiosity that was to be abhorred, dare to undo everything. With the best will in the world, he could not guarantee his posterity a beautiful sight after death had gnawed away at it to the end.

As fate would have it, less than two weeks later, a violent storm swept over Schilda, tearing tiles here and there from the roofs as if to check whether everyone, including every woman of course, was in the right bed, whirling a few horse-drawn carts through the air and, last but not least, toppling the huge old oak tree as if to see if there was any treasure to be found in that place.

It was a great shock when the first citizens of Schilda passed through the village the next day. The roots of the old oak had brought Uhlenspiegel's coffin back to light. The wooden structure sat enthroned in majestic silence at the foot of the fallen tree. It only took a short while for the mayor to reach the terrible place.

No one dared to open the coffin. Instead, they knocked timidly on the wood to find out whether Uhlenspiegel was still alive and would return their signal. Suddenly, as if by a miraculous hand, the coffin lid flew open. However, this was not due to a miraculous hand, but to a last gust of wind, because the storm had simply become too wild and wanted to see for itself what it had brought to light.

In the purple silk lining lay a skeleton whose outline even the wind was able to identify as a dog.

He was also a real dog, mocked one of the citizens of Schilda present, after everyone had recovered from the shock, in the end everything came to its proper order and in the bright shining daylight of the sun.

Shut your mouth or I'll shove my fist in it, the mayor scolded him. No one has the right to mock a dead man, especially since the deceased was an honorary citizen of Schilda, if you look at it the right way.

However, the explanation was simple, the mayor continued. On his wondrous journeys, he had traveled to a land where the inhabitants had found out what life was like, especially after death. Everything is an endless cycle of growth and decay and in the next round it could well happen that you return to this cycle as an animal. However, he was also amazed that Uhlenspiegel had consumed the impressive supply in such a short time and yet only a meagre skeleton remained. But what else could a man do when he was lying in a coffin all day with all the delicious things around him but eat, eat and eat again. But since Uhlenspiegel had taken the gold coins with him on his journey through the world of the dead, no one should be worried about him. He could live on those until he arrived in heaven, where there would be gold coins in abundance.

Since that time, the dogs of Schilda have been accorded a special reverence. This also made the inhabitants of Schilda citizens of the world.

There were cows in the land of pepper, snakes and camels in the land of pointed burial mounds, every country in the world needed an animal to identify itself with and what could be more obvious than to choose a dog in Schilda.

Quite a few people thought they recognized Uhlenspiegel's look when they looked into the eyes of a four-legged friend on future days and so Schilda turned into a paradise for dogs of every kind, the big ones as well as the small ones, the miserably crawling ones as well as the proudly upright walking ones, the four-legged ones as well as the two-legged or briefly three-legged ones. However, if you happened to come across a dog alone, it was not uncommon for this four-legged friend to be given a good kick up the backside in private and in memory of the lost gold coins.

Uhlenspiegel no longer minded. He enjoyed the delicacies he had been given and used the gold coins for what they were best suited to: a life of, let's put it more neutrally, a life of luxury. Where this life took place for someone who had already been nibbled away by death, is another story, which, as fate would have it, will be told on another occasion.

That is written in another book, but there are books everywhere on earth, even in Schilda and certainly in mysterious heaven. Everywhere but in hell, because in the sea of endless flames the black shadows of the spirit would not have lasted a second on the blooming/bloody white of the paper.

Index

1. Dangerous dream of gold
2. Nothing (–) makes you happy
3. Money stinks (doesn't stink)
4. White/wise portable stoves
5. Fairytale everyday life
6. Dry run
7. The black smouldering rose
8. House-stacked time
9. A strange unfortunate chain of events
10. Make one from two (by yourself)
11. Sweet post-Christmas decree
12. Death without end

Biography

After graduating from high school in Berlin, I studied medicine in Berlin and Munich and worked in medicine for around 40 years after my studies. I have been retired since the end of 2022. During my professional career I also wrote some manuscripts, a book for young people, children's books, novels and poems. Some have since been self-published.

In addition the author has published several novels in English translation:

Manu's Journey With Death
- A fugue through time

A life, narrated on several levels, accompanied in its tracks and followed by death. In some places, points of this life that have long since passed light up, a brief glowing breath where it pauses for a moment before it is dragged on by the stream of life and disappears somewhere, not without trace but forever. What remains? In any case, death, even if no one is interested in the remnants of this trace of life.

Chrystillian Christmas –
Christmas as usual ~~and~~ different

A goose on its flight to baking-oven land, chasing a golden angel's curl, encountering a mutant Christmas tree, an endless line of waiting stars, Santa's great-great-ancestor and, of course, Father Christmas himself, sitting on a cloud under whose shadow a boy is riding down from the peaks of the Andes, spreading the news of Christ's birth ... It could be like that, but it isn't quite, maybe a little, but just maybe. An Advent calendar of Christmas short stories, profound and loving, varied and multi-faceted, presented in a wonderful narrative style that will enchant even the adult reader. A fragrance-wrapped Christmas soufflé that can be eaten over 26+1 days, on each day of

Advent and Christmas plus New Year's Eve, or all at once, depending on the size of your appetite or Christmas taste ...

The Island of Figures
Youth Novel

A little girl in Japan receives a doll from her father for her birthday. When the girl is older, the doll is placed on the waves of the sea in a small boat. Apparently a tradition to mark the transition to a new phase of life into adulthood.

Some time later, another girl travels after her missing doll, and an exciting, adventurous journey begins with an unusual, surprising end.

Allegories
Short Stories Volume 1 -4

The following collection in 4 volumes contains just over 60 short stories, each short story is based on a biblical passage from the New Testament like a parable and is applied to our time. A short time to catch your breath, a short time perhaps to reflect, a short time perhaps to delve deeper. Although Christ used everyday life for his parables, they still leave a deep impression today. They are easy to remember with a hidden important message that we discover when we think about them.

Roxanna
And the Mysterious Monk

Detective Roxanna has solved her first case when life, or rather death, puts another case on her desk. This brings her into contact with a wealthy English gentleman at his country estate, who has amassed a considerable fortune with an unusual business idea. Among them is a complicated hunter, who is not only a little over-the-top in his language, and especially a monk who, with his incredible intuition, not only beats the inspector to it once.

Roxanna
The Fatal Secret of the Murder Books

It begins with a murder, a somewhat bizarre female detective, events that take place in Rome, England and France. A story that jumps back to the Middle Ages, runs on two tracks, two suspicious women and a dead man who suddenly appears one night to one of the two suspects. A tangled criminal string that seems to have been partially untangled by diligent endeavours — only to become even more tangled in the next moment and finally, seemingly lying in front of you untangled in a perfectly straight line.

Uhlenspiegel with the Schilda Citizens
Volume 1 - 3

Uhlenspiegel, the lone warrior, armed with an army of mischievous thoughts, encounters a village full of Schilda citizens who are less armed, or rather, armed with different thoughts. Uhlenspiegel's premise: "Where money is at stake, it's good to be good!" And so he mischievously plays out his insights on the Schilda citizens who, with their naive way of thinking, are the appropriate antagonists. Does such an encounter make sense? Amusing and entertaining, in any case!